PENNY McKINLAY grew up in Cheshire and read English at Oxford University. She began her career as a news and show business journalist on the *Daily Mirror* and *Daily Mail*, and subsequently joined TV AM as a producer. She is now Head of the News Features department at Sky News.
Penny's previous children's books include *The Prisoner* and *Escape from Germany* (Watts), and *The Toy Shop Dog* (HarperCollins). Penny lives in London and is married with two children – one of whose first ballet lessons inspired this book!

GRAHAM PERCY was born and raised in New Zealand. He studied Graphic Design at the Royal College of Art, and has been an illustrator for over 20 years. His previous titles include *The Cock, The Mouse and the Little Red Hen* and *A Cup of Starshine* (Walker Books), *Children's Favourite Animal Fables* (David Bennett Books) and *The Wind in the Willows* (Pavilion Books). Graham lives in London.

To Mum and Dad — P.M.
To Brittany — G.P.

Elephants Don't Do Ballet copyright © Frances Lincoln Limited 1997
Text copyright © Penny McKinlay 1997
Illustrations copyright © Graham Percy 1997

First published in Great Britain in 1997 by
Frances Lincoln Limited, 4 Torriano Mews
Torriano Avenue, London NW5 2RZ

First paperback edition 1998

British Library Cataloguing in Publication Data
available on request

ISBN 0-7112-1109-4 hardback
ISBN 0-7112-1130-2 paperback

Set in 17/22pt Administer

Printed in Hong Kong
9 8 7 6 5

ELEPHANTS
don't do
ballet

Penny McKinlay
Illustrated by Graham Percy

FRANCES LINCOLN

One Christmas, Esmeralda was given a musical box with a tiny gold ballerina on top. When the music played, the ballerina twirled elegantly round on one leg.

"I want to be a ballerina," said Esmeralda.

Her brother Ernest snorted into his bucket of milk. "Elephants don't do ballet!"

"Now, Ernest," said Mummy.

Esmeralda tied a knot in her trunk. "I want to be a ballerina!"

Mummy sighed. "Yes, dear. I'll see about lessons."

Next day, Mummy rang the ballet school.
"She'll need a leotard," said the ballet teacher.
"A pink one. And pink ballet shoes. Be here at six o'clock sharp."

The man in the dance shop looked worried when he saw Esmeralda. Mummy curled her trunk and coughed delicately.

"Um, Large, would you say?"

But even Extra Extra Large didn't fit.

Esmeralda tied a knot in her trunk and stamped her foot. The shop shook.

"I think we'd better go, dear," said Mummy.

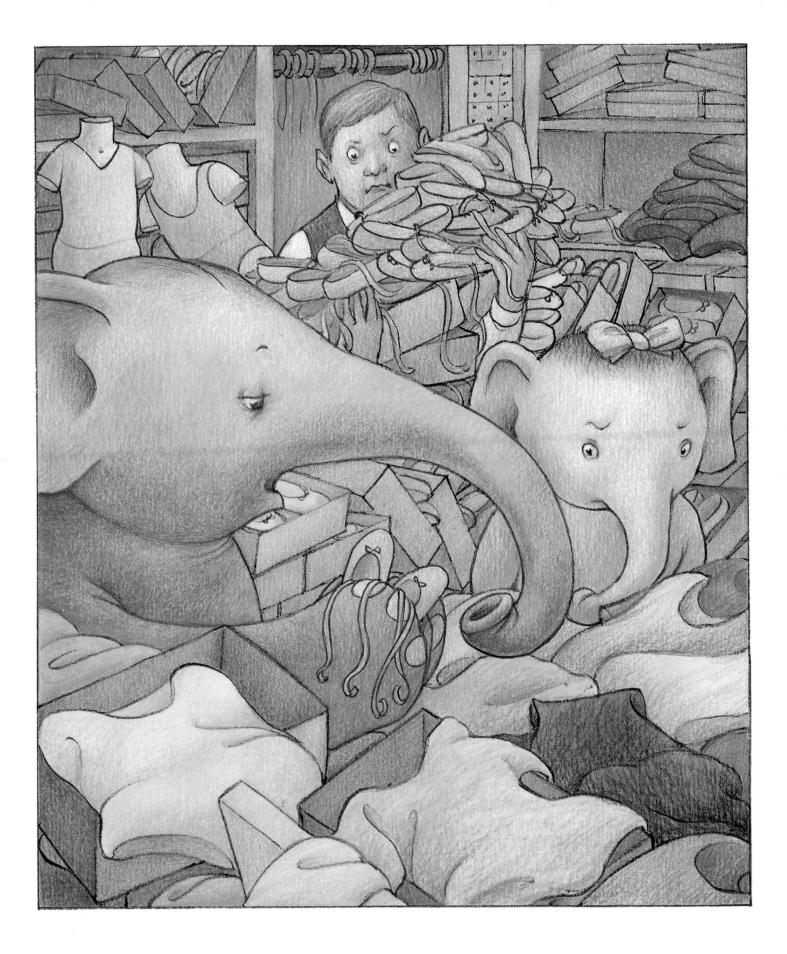

On the way home they passed a furniture store.
A sign in the window caught Mummy's eye.

MR MIRACLE'S CHAIR COVERS
STRETCH TO FIT THE LARGEST SEAT!

"Do you have those in pink?" enquired Mummy.

They did – and they fitted perfectly. Esmeralda did
a delighted twirl and the chandelier shook.
   They even had pink footstool covers to match.
   "We'll take four!" Mummy trumpeted in triumph.

Shortly before six they arrived at the ballet class.
Silence fell as Esmeralda trundled in.
Someone giggled. "She's fat!" said a small voice.

Esmeralda tied a knot in her trunk.
  "Ignore them, Esmeralda," said Mummy. "And
do untie your trunk, dear. It doesn't look nice."

The lesson started. Mummy wrapped her trunk tightly around her eyes and ears.

"First, girls," said the teacher, "we shall learn to point our toes. Right foot, clap, left foot, clap. Off we go!"

Esmeralda got in a terrible tangle. She pointed both right feet at once, and capsized.

The ballet teacher called out, "Try pointing your back feet and clapping with your front, Esmeralda. See you all next week, girls!"

The next week, Mummy folded her ear-flaps over her eyes.

"Today, girls, we shall learn to trot like little ponies," said the ballet teacher.

The class trotted in a circle.

"Now, girls, we shall gallop!" cried the teacher.

There were muffled screams as Esmeralda lumbered into a gallop. The ballet teacher hauled the girls out from under Esmeralda's feet.

"In future, Esmeralda, stick to a trot," said the teacher. "See you next week, girls!"

The next week, Mummy wore ear-plugs and did a crossword.

"Today, girls, we shall learn to twirl," said the teacher.

But when Esmeralda twirled, her trunk wrapped itself so tightly round her neck, she couldn't breathe. By the time she got it untangled, her face was blue.

"Next time, Esmeralda, try holding a wand in your trunk," said the teacher. "See you next week, girls!"

The next week, Mummy wore headphones and did her knitting.

"Today, girls, we shall learn to jump!" said the teacher. "One at a time, I think," she added nervously, looking at Esmeralda.

Esmeralda soared up... and crashed down on to a
loose plank. The ballerina on the other end flew up
to the roof.

"Perhaps more of a skip, Esmeralda?" suggested
the teacher, fetching a ladder. "Six o'clock next
week, girls!"

The next week, Mummy turned her back and read
the newspaper.
  "This week, girls, we shall reach up and pick stars,"
said the ballet teacher.

Esmeralda stretched her stumpy little legs, up, up...
and tottered heavily back on to the grand piano.

While they waited for an ambulance to take the
pianist away, the teacher said: "Try using your trunk
to pick stars, Esmeralda. Now remember, girls, next
week is our show!"

At last it was the night of the show.
The music began.
The curtain started to rise. And stopped.
It rose a little more. And stopped.
Esmeralda's two back feet were planted firmly on the bottom of the curtain.

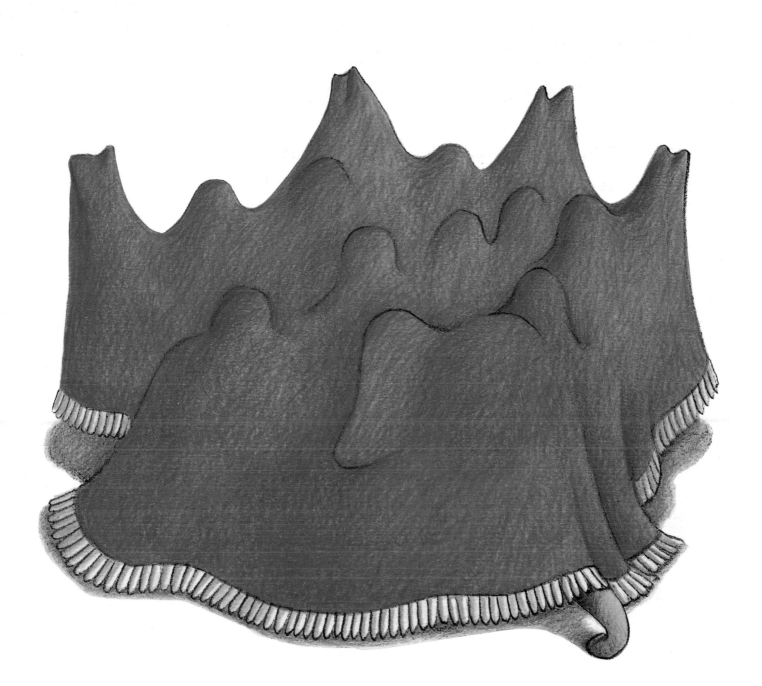

"Move your feet, Esmeralda!" hissed the teacher.
Too late. There was a loud rip – and the curtain
came crashing down, burying Esmeralda and all the
little ballerinas in an orange velvet heap.

The a trunk emerged from under the curtain.
With a heave, Esmeralda rose and twirled the
curtain gracefully above her head, while the little
ballerinas clung to the edges like stars.

Esmeralda lowered the curtain and the ballerinas
danced around her as she stood with the orange
velvet curtain draped about her, like a queen.

In a grand finale, each little ballerina leaped lightly on to Esmeralda's trunk and pirouetted perfectly, like the little ballerina on the Christmas musical box.

Afterwards, the audience clapped as if they would never stop.

"Well done, Esmeralda!" cried the ballet teacher.

Mummy hugged Esmeralda tightly with her trunk.

Ernest tugged Esmeralda's tail. "You were right," he said. "Elephants *can* do ballet."

On the way home, they passed the ice-skating
rink. Outside was a picture of a lady skating.
Esmeralda's eyes glinted.

"I want to be an ice-skater!" she said.

Ernest choked on his bubble gum.

"Elephants can't..."

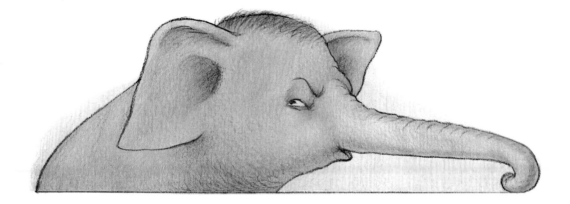

"I want to be an ice-skater!"

Esmeralda stamped. The pavement cracked.

Mummy sighed. "Yes, dear," she said.

"I'll see about lessons."

MORE PICTURE BOOKS IN PAPERBACK
FROM FRANCES LINCOLN

MISSING!
Jonathan Langley

Every day, Lupin the cat is there to meet Daisy when she comes home from nursery.
On the first day of the holidays, Lupin waits for Daisy as usual, but Daisy doesn't appear !
Follow Lupin and Daisy's hilarious adventures as they set out to search for each other
in this delightful and charmingly illustrated story.

Suitable for National Curriculum English – Reading, Key Stage 1
Scottish Guidelines English Language – Reading, Level A

ISBN 0-7112-1543-X

SIMON SAYS
Shen Roddie
Illustrated by Sally Anne Lambert

Simon Pig has the perfect plan to make Sally Goose do all his work. "Let's play Simon Says!"
he says to her. "You do whatever Simon Says." Soon poor Sally is rushing
around planting carrots, making a scarecrow and even clipping Simon's nails.
But when it's finally Sally's turn to play, she thinks of a great way to get her own back!

Suitable for National Curriculum English – Reading, Key Stage 1
Scottish Guidelines English Language – Reading, Level A

ISBN 0-7112-1532-4

COPY ME, COPYCUB
Richard Edwards
Illustrated by Susan Winter

Copycub learns everything by copying his mother.
A beautiful story alive with warmth and humour.

Suitable for National Curriculum English – Reading, Key Stage 1
Scottish Guidelines English Language – Reading, Level A

ISBN 0-7112-1460-3

Frances Lincoln titles are available from all good bookshops.